lex--
5.8
6 pts

The
Great Christmas
Kidnaping Caper

THE
Great Christmas
Kidnaping Caper

Jean Van Leeuwen
pictures by Steven Kellogg

Dial Books for Young Readers
New York

Typography by Barbara Hennessy
Printed in the United States of America
COBE
11 13 15 14 12 10

Library of Congress Cataloging in Publication Data
Van Leeuwen, Jean. The great Christmas kidnaping caper.
[1. Mice—Fiction.   2. Christmas stories]
I. Kellogg, Steven.   II. Title.
PZ7.V3273Gr.   [Fic]   75-9201
ISBN 0-8037-5415-9   ISBN 0-8037-5416-7 lib. bdg.

For
my mother and father
who still believe
in Santa Claus

Contents

The
Great Christmas
Kidnaping Caper

1

I Discover
the World's Largest Store

I am standing on the corner of Broadway and 34th
Street. It is getting dark, and the wind is chill. In it
there is the smell of winter. A snowflake lands on
my nose, and I shiver. I edge a little closer to the
man selling hot chestnuts who shares my corner.
His fire warms my front, but my tail is still cold.

I look around for a place to spend the night. In
warmer weather I would not be so choosy. I would
sleep under a park bench or in the alley behind my
favorite Chinese restaurant. I consider some of my
other haunts—a trash barrel next to the vending

machines in the subway station, an all-night theater on 42nd Street, the Automat. Or I could visit my old gang at the cheese store. But that's too far uptown, and besides, tonight I am in the mood for something different, something more luxurious.

It is getting crowded on my corner. People are hurrying out of stores and offices, heading for warm apartments and hot dinners. The thought of hot dinners reminds me that I have not eaten since this morning. It was a piece of stale bagel from a trash can outside a delicatessen: very hard on the molars. The life of a mouse living by his wits alone in the city is not an easy one.

A couple more snowflakes melt on my ears, and I pull up the collar of my raincoat. Then I notice it: a revolving door out of which people are streaming. It must be the entrance to a store because they are carrying packages—all sizes and strange shapes wrapped up in red and green paper. The packages look interesting. They might be edible. I decide to go in.

I sidle over to the door and wait. With revolving doors, timing is the most important thing. This I

4

know from sad experience. The door is spinning fast, and I notice that everyone is coming out, no one is going in. It must be closing time. Finally there are fewer people. And then comes what I have been waiting for: a weak little old lady who can barely push the door around. I slip in, remembering to move fast and keep my tail tucked in. In a moment I've made it. I'm inside.

Right away I duck into the shadow of the nearest counter. I let the warmth sink into my bones, and again I wait, for people to finish leaving the store. Feet march past my hiding place. I hear cash registers ringing, bags of change clinking. Then a voice over a loudspeaker announces: "The store is now closing. Please complete your purchases. Thank you for shopping at Macy's, the world's largest store." The world's largest store! I have hit the jackpot. I may even decide to stay all winter.

Fewer and fewer feet come past my hiding place. I see a man in a blue uniform locking the revolving door. It looks like a cop, and I quickly duck back into the shadows. I am not fond of cops. They are always interrupting my meals. And I have a dent in my tail from a nightstick that just missed my head in the alley behind the Chinese restaurant.

While I'm looking this cop over, a sudden gust of wind almost blows me off my feet. I look up to see a giant plastic cloth descending over the entire counter. To keep the dust off, I figure. It almost dusts me off. At the same time the lights grow dim, and voices call to each other: "Good night, Rose," "See you all tomorrow," "Who's taking the subway uptown?"

And then at last the store is quiet. Everyone seems to have gone home. Cautiously I poke my nose out, looking for the cop. But he has disappeared too. So I step from my hiding place to have a look around.

Rows and rows of counters, all covered with plastic cloths. They look spooky in the dim light, like the deserted mansion in a horror movie I saw last week. Under the cloths I can make out all kinds of merchandise: ladies' hats, handbags, shoes, perfume, men's shirts, umbrellas, sweaters, neckties. Nothing here for me. I begin to wonder if I've hit the jackpot after all.

In the quiet I notice a low hum, like some kind of machine. Slipping from counter to counter, I finally locate the sound. It is an escalator. Of course the world's largest store has more than one floor. The food is probably upstairs. I decide to go up.

Riding an escalator requires even more skill and daring than going through a revolving door. Escalators are usually crowded with people, and there are high-heeled shoes and heavy packages and sharp umbrellas to watch out for. There are also cracks through which a mouse could fall and never be seen again. But I have this escalator all to myself. I'm having such a good time on it that when I get to the second floor I keep on going, all the way up as far as it goes.

Pianos. That's the first thing I see when I get off. I don't play so I'm not interested. Beyond the pianos are miles and miles of sofas and chairs and chests of drawers and tables and desks and bookcases. And beds. I've never seen so many beds. Looking at them, I suddenly feel very sleepy. I bounce on a few of the mattresses and even stretch out on one for a little snooze. But I can't sleep with that gnawing empty feeling in my stomach. I decide to try the next floor down.

I step off the escalator into the china department. There are tables set with lace tablecloths, plates, glasses, silverware, even salt and pepper shakers. Only one thing is missing: food. I am just taking a desperate lick at a plate with some painted-on fruit when I smell it. I can't believe my nose and I sniff again. *Cheese!*

Leaping off the table, I follow the aroma through the clock department, the picture frame department, and a jungle of trees and plants and flowers. I'm so hungry that I take a nibble of a leaf as I go by. Yuck —plastic! And then, there it is: a delicatessen right in the middle of the world's largest store.

I go straight to the cheeses. It has been a long time since I had a choice of all my favorites: port wine cheddar, Gruyère, fontina, Tilsit, imported Swiss. I take a nibble from each one, then I spot Camembert and Liederkranz and Vermont cheddar. By the time I've had a bite of each, I am getting a little bit full. But there is Gouda and Port Salut and Gorgonzola and Limburger. When I have tasted all of these, I am so stuffed I can hardly move. I can see rows of other intriguing delicacies waiting to be sampled, but they will have to wait for another day. Right now all I want to do is sleep.

I don't want to be discovered snoozing among the cheeses when the store opens in the morning, so, stashing a hunk of imported Swiss under my hat, I make my way back to the down escalator. Somewhere in the world's largest store there must be a perfect hideaway for a mouse who's thinking of spending the winter. On the next floor down I can see nothing but curtains. This is not the place. On the floor below there are piles of blankets and sheets and towels. I keep on riding.

The first thing to hit my eye on the next floor are rows and rows of television sets. This looks more promising. I could watch movies every night like in the old days when I used to live in a movie theater. I decide to give this floor a closer inspection. Next to the TV sets are refrigerators and stoves and washing machines. I consider moving into a washing machine. But what if someone turned it on for a demonstration? I have a feeling I wouldn't like being spun dry. I move on to the luggage department. No one would think of looking for a mouse in a suitcase. But what if someone bought me? I walk on.

Then suddenly I find myself in a whole new world. Everything in it seems to have shrunk to my size. There are tiny racing cars and dump trucks and buses and motorcycles. There are airplanes and fire engines and whole fleets of boats. There are airports and schools and parking garages and farms and even a miniature merry-go-round. I take a spin on the merry-go-round, and when I look up, a whole shelf full of animals is watching me: bears and tigers, monkeys and giraffes, ducks and rabbits. I get ready to make a run for it, but they don't move or even blink an eye. Then I realize that they are stuffed, and I know where I am. I have found the toy department.

I look over the piles of games and puzzles and painting sets and tea sets. I see dolls of all sizes, puppets, building blocks, race tracks, model airplanes. And then on a huge table I discover the best toy of all. It is a little train on a track that goes around in circles and through tunnels and over bridges. It has

10

a town with houses the size of Crackerjack boxes and people smaller than mice. There are little cows eating grass in a field and ducks swimming in a real pond. At one end I see a box with rows of switches and lights and buttons. I go over to study it. While I am trying to figure out what all these switches are for, I accidentally lean on one. Suddenly the train backs up into the station. Aha, now I understand. I push a button, and like magic the train stops. This is easy. I flip another switch and it goes forward, light flashing and smoke puffing out of its chimney. When it gets to me, I think, "Why not?" and I jump on board.

I'm off on one of the wildest rides of my career. Whistle blowing, the train careens around curves, chugs up hills, and races over bridges. I hang onto my hat as we brush past trees and telephone poles and speed past grassy fields. Then up ahead looms a dark tunnel, and I duck just in time. Around and around we go until I am so dizzy I can hardly see. But I'm laughing and telling the engine, "Faster, faster!"

Then just as suddenly as my ride began, it is over.

The engine jerks to a halt so fast that I am thrown off. Even before I open my eyes, I have an idea I haven't landed in the best place. I feel a little damp. I open one eye and find that I am in the duck pond. But worse than that, I can make out something moving toward me. It is something very big holding a flashlight and wearing a blue uniform: the cop!

In a flash I am out of the duck pond, off the table, and racing across the floor. Wildly I look for some place to hide. I pass the dolls, the doll furniture, the doll carriages—and suddenly I stop short. Way up on the top shelf, tucked away in a dark corner as if everyone had forgotten it, is a white house with green shutters. Without stopping to think it over, I climb up, duck inside, and slam the door.

I wait, my heart hammering, for the flashlight to find my hiding place. But everything is dark and quiet. I think maybe I have given him the slip. After a minute I peek out the window to make sure. He is standing at the next counter, shining his flashlight on the shelf of stuffed animals. I see him shake his head. Then his light moves away and disappears down the escalator.

I breathe a long sigh of relief. Looking around me for the first time, I notice that I am standing next to a flight of stairs. I am almost too tired to climb them, but I make it, and at the top I find a room with a canopy-covered bed just my size. Wearily I crawl under the covers, and in a minute I am asleep.

2
I Send for My Gang

I have a wonderful dream. I dream I am curled up in a real bed, all snug and warm, with a patchwork quilt pulled up under my chin. There are no winter winds whistling around my ears, no snow or sleet soaking my fur, no cats, rats, or cops waiting to chase me.

When I open my eyes, I am curled up in a real bed, all snug and warm, with a patchwork quilt pulled up under my chin. I think I must still be dreaming. But then I remember last night and I smile.

Looking around, I see ruffled white curtains at the windows and soft rugs on the floor. There is a bedside table, a rocking chair, a lamp, even a place to hang my hat. There is no doubt about it: I have discovered a house built just for a mouse.

It's the perfect place to spend the winter. Besides all the comforts of my own little house, there is plenty of food just an escalator ride away, TV to while away the long winter nights, the electric train for excitement. And with the cop around, just enough danger to keep life interesting. Yes, I have made my decision. I will not set foot out of the store until spring.

With that settled, I yawn, stretch, and turn over to go back to sleep. It is then I notice that my location has one disadvantage I hadn't thought of. The toy department is not exactly the quietest corner of the store. In fact, it is quite noisy. I am too comfortable to move, but on the other hand I know from experience that a mouse can't be too careful. So I climb out of bed and go to the window to see what is going on.

The first thing I see is this fat guy in a red suit. He's got a long white beard and bright pink cheeks

16

and a funny-looking hat, and he's sitting on a huge chair like a king on a throne. All around the chair are blue-green fake pine trees with candy canes hanging on them. There's a little kid on the fat guy's knee and the kid's mother is standing nearby smiling like crazy and music is playing and the fat guy is chuckling in a hearty voice: "Merrrrrry Christmas! Ho ho ho!" It's the most peculiar thing I've ever seen.

At first glance, though, it doesn't look dangerous, not with everyone smiling. I study the situation for a few more minutes. The fat guy talks to the kid for a while, then he gives him a pat on the head and hands him a lollipop. The kid walks away smiling, and another kid climbs up on the fat guy's knee, and the whole performance starts all over again. I notice there is a long line of kids and parents waiting to go through this routine with the fat guy. Why they would bother I can't imagine. The only explanation I can think of is he must be giving away the best lollipops in town.

After watching awhile, I get bored. Who can stand all that smiling and head-patting and ho-ho-hoing? It's so jolly it's sickening.

So I move over to the other window. From here I can see more action. There must be a million shoppers in the toy department, mostly women with their arms full of packages, but also a lot of kids trying out all the toys. A bunch of them are crowded around the table watching my electric train race around the track. Some kids are testing wind-up toys on another table, others are looking at airplane models. Closer to me a little girl, all dressed up in a red velvet coat, has her nose pressed to the glass case where the dolls are.

Watching her, I slowly realize the terrible truth. This house wasn't built for a mouse at all; it was built for a doll. And then a worse thought comes to me: what if that little girl's mother decides to buy her a dollhouse? *This* dollhouse.

Keep calm, I tell myself. Don't panic. Keeping a cool head, I consider the situation. Luckily my house is up high where no kid could reach it. And it does seem very dusty and old-fashioned. Anyone who wanted a dollhouse would most likely choose the modern ranch-style model that I can see next-door to mine. Just to be sure, though, I make a note to

18

gather some extra dust and cobwebs and spread them around to make sure my house doesn't attract customers.

I can see now that I will have to keep my eyes and ears open. And I won't be able to leave my house in the daytime when the store is open. It is much too dangerous. But that doesn't bother me. I'll sleep all day and play all night.

Climbing back into bed, I unwrap the snack of cheese I had tucked away in my hat. I lie there nibbling and dozing and listening to the music the store has thoughtfully provided for my listening pleasure. This is the life. If only my old gang could see me now.

I think of Raymond and Fats and the good old days when we led a life of crime in the Bijou Theater. Watching hundreds of gangster movies convinced me that I was meant for bigger things than just raiding the popcorn stand and the candy machines. I trained my gang well, gave them their names (Raymond the Rat to make him think fierce; Fats the Fuse because of his fondness for explosives), and when they were ready, we pulled off our first big job: robbing a cheese store. After this triumph I wanted to move on to more adventures, but Raymond and Fats could not be budged. Now they lead the easy life, their every need provided for by the kind-hearted old man who owns the cheese shop. They have gotten soft. Adventure has gone out of their lives.

It is time I helped them live again. I snap my fingers. That's it! Why not send for my gang to move in with me here? There is plenty of room in my house. Fats could use a change from his diet of cheese and more cheese. The delicatessen would drive him crazy. And Raymond, who is the scholarly type, would go for the book department. With the long winter ahead, he could probably read through an entire set of encyclopedias. Yes, I'll do it. I'll send for my gang.

Then it occurs to me that without my gang, I have no one to send. What a comedown for a leader. This is definitely not the way things are done in the gangster movies. But I have no choice. I will have to go myself.

So that very night at closing time I do what I

promised myself I would not do until spring. I slip out of my house, jump off my shelf and, mingling with the crowd of shoppers, make my way to the down escalator. It's a hazardous ride, dodging boots and shopping bags, but I am nimble. Following the crowd, I take a fast whirl through the revolving door, then scurry down the steps to the subway. The rest is easy. I catch the last car of the BMT, change to the IRT, and in minutes I'm at the back door of the cheese shop.

Slipping through the crack that Fats long ago enlarged to mouse size, I say, "Greetings, gang."

There is no answer.

I tiptoe over to the cheese carton where Raymond and Fats make their home and peer inside. All I can see is an old motheaten gray sweater at one end and some newspapers at the other. It looks like no one is at home. Then I notice that one sleeve of the sweater is snoring. And there is a rustle behind one of the newspapers.

"Ahem," I say loudly, and Raymond puts down his *New York Globe*.

"Oh, it's you, Marvin," he says.

I march over to the sweater, reach into the sleeve, and drag Fats out by the tail. "Wha-what's the idea," he mumbles, rubbing his eyes sleepily. Then he opens them. "Oh, hi, Marvin," he says.

"Gang," I announce, "I have come to offer you the opportunity of a lifetime."

Fats blinks at me, then his head sags to his chest and his eyes close again. I notice that Raymond is sneaking a peek at the financial page out of the corner of his eye. My gang hasn't just gone soft, they are totally limp. I can see I'm going to have to retrain them—make them lean and quick and tough like me.

For starters I decide to remind them again of who's boss. Snatching Fats's tail, I give it the old torture twist that I perfected from watching a lot of prison movies. "Y-y-yes, Marvin," he stammers.

"Marvin what?" I demand.

"M-m-merciless Marvin the Magnificent," he says grudgingly.

"That's better."

Raymond has put down his newspaper. At last I have their full attention.

"Gang," I begin again, "I have come to offer you the opportunity of a lifetime." Then I describe to them my beautiful setup in the world's largest store. "So," I say in conclusion, "how would you like to get away from it all for a little winter vacation?"

There is total silence.

Raymond is stroking his whiskers as he always does when he is thinking. Finally he says slowly, "It was good of you to think of us, Marvin, but we don't need a vacation. We are on vacation all the time.

Mr. Sammartino is very good to us, you know. We have everything we need right here."

"Everything," agrees Fats, popping a crumb of cheese into his mouth. He yawns and edges toward the sleeve.

I yank him back by the tail. I came prepared for this. I knew it might take a little persuasion to pry them loose from the soft life.

"It is true that you have a comfortable setup here," I concede. "But everyone needs a change now and then. Variety is the spice of life, and besides, without a little adventure life isn't worth living." I am getting warmed up now. "Adventure is good for the brain, it tones up the blood, it trims down the waistline." I glance significantly at Fats's ample stomach.

He looks offended, and they both look unconvinced. I can see that I'm going to have to use my most powerful ammunition.

So I say casually to Raymond, "I just happened to notice that the book department has a complete set of the *Encyclopaedia Britannica.*"

"Really?" I can see Raymond is interested in spite of himself. His eyes have a far-away look as he says,

"Once someone left Volume Fourteen in the movie theater. I remember it well: Salamander to Velocipede."

While this is sinking in, I turn to Fats. "Not only does the world's largest store have a bed department where you can try out a different mattress every night, but it also has the world's largest delicatessen. Imagine it. All your favorite cheeses *plus* your choice of delicacies from all over the world. Imported butter cookies, sesame crackers, anchovies, artichokes, pickles, marmalade, honey—"

I stop because Fats is looking at me with an odd expression. "Did you say . . . pickles?"

I nod, and a huge ridiculous smile spreads over his face. "I remember the last pickle I had," he says dreamily. "I found it in a bag with half a bologna sandwich in the next to the last row of the balcony."

Now I know I have them.

"Come on, gang," I say. "Let's start packing."

3

I Make the Acquaintance of Santa Claus

I am sprawled out on the double bed in Raymond's new room, nibbling on a slice of muenster with caraway seeds and watching him unpack.

Unpacking has taken Raymond most of the day. That is because Raymond the Rat is a saver. Over the months he has lived in the cheese shop, he has collected all kinds of things that people threw away or accidentally dropped, and he has insisted on bringing most of this junk with him. Now he is carefully arranging it all in two tall chests of drawers. I watch as everything but his tail disappears inside the old argyle sock that serves as his suitcase. He emerges clutching two overcoat buttons as if they were emeralds and places them in the bottom drawer next to a comb with broken teeth, three pencil stubs, a hairnet, two lipsticks, a stick of old chewing gum, a few crayons, a broken shoelace, four Band-aids, a baby's rattle, and his pocket dictionary.

"What is all this junk good for anyway?" I ask.

"You never know when it will come in handy," Raymond replies, disappearing into the sock again. He believes in being ready for any emergency.

I glance over at the window where Fats has been whiling away the hours until we can make our first raid on the delicatessen by watching the action in the toy department.

"Is that crazy fat guy in the red suit still there?" I ask lazily.

"He's not fat," Fats says in a hurt voice, looking down at his own stomach. "My mother always called me her pleasingly plump little dumpling."

Raymond has just removed a key ring and two flashlight batteries from his sock. "Of course Santa Claus is still there, Marvin," he says. "He'll be there every day till Christmas."

"Of course," I say. So that's who the fat guy is. And that explains why the toy department is so crowded. Everyone is buying toys for Christmas.

"Who is Santa Claus?" Fats asks.

"What a dumb question," I say with a scowl. "Everyone knows who Santa Claus is. Uh—you tell him, Raymond."

Raymond stops his unpacking, takes off his spectacles, polishes them carefully with a tissue, and puts them back on. I can tell he is about to make a speech.

"Santa Claus," he begins in his most school-teacherish voice, "is the spirit of the Christmas season. Legend has it that he makes his home at the North Pole where, with the help of his elves, he makes toys for children. Then on Christmas Eve he hitches his reindeer to his sleigh, fills it with toys, and sets out to deliver presents to every child in the world. No one ever sees him come or go, but when the children wake up on Christmas morning, there under the Christmas tree they find the gifts Santa Claus has left for them." Raymond pauses and then adds, "So you see, Santa Claus represents the joy of giving, and especially giving to children, that people feel at Christmas time."

This is without a doubt the most sickeningly sweet story I have ever heard. "Bah humbug," I snort.

But Fats has that dreamy look like he gets when he talks about pickles. "Imagine that," he sighs with a foolish grin. "The spirit of Christmas. And he is pleasingly plump like me."

I decide to bring him down to earth. "That was a pretty good story," I tell Raymond. "But how come Santa Claus is here at Macy's instead of at the North Pole getting ready for this big free giveaway?"

"That's a good question," Raymond says, tugging at his whiskers thoughtfully. "I've done some reading on the subject, and as I understand it, the real Santa Claus *is* at the North Pole preparing for Christmas Eve. The Santas we see in stores and on the streets are his assistants. They are here to find out from children what they would like the real Santa Claus to bring them for Christmas."

"Hmmmmmph," I sniff. "Silliest thing I ever heard of."

But Fats has fallen for this Santa Claus fairy tale hook, line, and sinker. All afternoon while I snooze and Raymond's chests of drawers grow more and

29

more stuffed with junk, Fats keeps sticking his head out the window to see what Santa Claus is doing.

"He's bouncing a baby on his knee," he reports happily. "Everyone is smiling." And later, "He's giving a little girl a candy cane from the Christmas tree. Oh, I love Christmas trees! Last year at the cheese store Mr. Sammartino trimmed a real live little tree with strings of popcorn just for us. It was beautiful. And it tasted good too."

"These trees aren't real," I snap without opening my eyes. "And get your head inside before someone sees you."

When I awaken a few minutes later and glance over at the windowsill, all I can see is Fat's hind feet and tail. The rest of him is on its way out the window.

I leap across the room and haul him back in. "What's the idea?" I demand. "Do you want to get us discovered and thrown out in the snow?"

Fats looks sheepish. "I only wanted to get a better look," he protests, rubbing a bumped elbow. "Santa Claus left his chair and was walking this way. The children have gone so the store must be closing."

"Let's hope he wasn't looking your way," I tell

30

him. "A mouse of your size would be hard to miss."

Raymond looks up from sorting his collection of safety pins, paperclips, collar buttons, and subway tokens. He looks a bit worried. Fats is looking guilty. I decide it is time to change the subject.

"Fats, my boy," I say, "the moment you've been waiting for is at hand. It's time to raid the pickle jar."

I awake the next morning with a big smile on my face. Thanks to my leadership, last night's raid went like clockwork. There wasn't a sign of the cop, and we were quiet and discreet, leaving no telltale crumbs or footprints behind. Fats had more than his share of pickles—kosher dills, sweet pickles, bread and butter pickles, watermelon pickles, pickled artichoke hearts—and I discovered a taste treat of my own: caviar! The memory of it lingers deliciously on my tongue. Sweet, succulent, slightly salty Iranian black caviar. Five dollars an ounce. I couldn't resist making off with a whole jar, which is waiting for me in the kitchen right now. The thought of it makes me jump out of bed.

I find Raymond and Fats at the kitchen table. Fats is not looking quite himself. For a moment I can't put my finger on it. Then I realize what it is. He is not eating anything.

"What's wrong? Don't you feel well?" I ask.

Fats shakes his head mournfully. "I think I ate too many pickles."

Raymond looks up. "There is something here you should see, Marvin," he says. "I found it just inside the door when I came downstairs."

In the middle of the table is a crumpled piece of paper. I recognize the label right away from our old days in the movie theater. It is a Snickers candy wrapper. Raymond unfolds it, and inside is an oatmeal cookie.

"Obviously," Raymond says slowly, "someone knows we are here."

I nod. "Obviously."

My first thought is that the game is up. We will have to leave the store. And just when I've discovered caviar.

"Probably," Raymond goes on, twirling his whiskers thoughtfully, "it is Santa Claus. He must have seen Fats yesterday."

I glare at Fats. He can't even look out a window without falling out. It is all his fault I will never taste caviar again. Why did I ever let him join my gang anyway?

"We'll move out tonight," I decide. "You two can go back to the cheese store. I'll get through the winter somehow."

Raymond doesn't answer. He twirls his whiskers faster as he thinks over the situation. At last he says, "It is true, Marvin, that someone—presumably Santa Claus—knows we are here. But he may not mean us any harm. Rather than calling the store manager or the police, he has left us food."

I hadn't thought of it that way. "You mean," I say, "he wants to be friends?"

"Exactly."

"Hmmmm." My first thought is that *I* don't want to be friends. I, Merciless Marvin, can take care of myself. But on the other hand, this Santa Claus character who is soft-hearted enough to let little kids climb all over him and stick their lollipops in his beard is probably soft-hearted enough to provide us with a lot of oatmeal cookies. And I've never been one to turn down a free meal.

"Okay," I say, making a fast, firm decision like a leader should, "we'll do it. We'll be his friends."

34

4

I Suspect Foul Play

Now that we are friends with Santa Claus, life is even more beautiful. Every morning he leaves us a snack wrapped up in a Snickers wrapper. Sometimes it is a piece of a candy bar, sometimes an oatmeal cookie, a doughnut, or even a cheese danish. Raymond, who gets up early to read his encyclopedia, reports that when Santa shoves the candy wrapper inside the door he whispers, "Good morning, my little friends." A true softy, this Santa Claus.

At noon Raymond brings our snack to our rooms to start off the day. After that we have our afternoon

35

naps; then when the store closes, we go into action. Every night we raid the delicatessen, trying such interesting gourmet delights as kumquats (so-so), herring in cream sauce (not bad), olives stuffed with baby onions (delicious), and Chinese fortune cookies (good to read but dull to eat). We get to know the schedule by which the cop makes his rounds and keep a safe distance away. After our evening meal we watch old movies on TV or test out new toys in the toy department. I take my gang for a spin on my electric train. Or Fats and I race each other in fancy sports cars while Raymond plays educational games all by himself. One night I discover a "Detective's Disguise Kit," and while I am seeing how I would look in a fake mustache, rubber nose, and sunglasses, Fats finds fingerpaints. We have a lot of cleaning up to do after he finishes a portrait of Santa Claus for his room. Another night the three of us try our hands at a little music: Raymond on xylophone, Fats on triangle, and me, Marvin the Magnificent, on drums. Life is truly beautiful.

Then one morning a very strange thing happens. When I wake up and reach for my morning snack from Santa Claus, there is nothing there.

I open my eyes. No, there is nothing on my bedside table. I look over at Raymond. He is sitting in
my rocking chair reading the *New York Globe,*
which one of the salesclerks discards in a certain
trash can each morning before the store opens.

"What's the idea?" I demand. "Who ate my
breakfast?"

"Santa didn't leave us anything today," Raymond answers apologetically. "He hasn't come to work this morning."

Fats is peering dejectedly out the window. "Maybe he's sick," he suggests. "Maybe he ate too many pickles and got a stomachache."

Raymond puts down his newspaper. "Nobody seems to know if he's sick or not. I heard a salesperson say he'd probably be here in a few minutes, but that was an hour ago. All the children are still waiting."

I listen. I can hear someone singing on the loudspeaker about a reindeer with a cold in his nose. And even louder than that, people shouting and laughing. There must be a lot of kids out there.

"It's strange that he hasn't called," Raymond says, looking a little worried.

It *is* strange. Another hour goes by, and still Santa Claus doesn't show up. Finally the manager of the toy department puts up a sign in front of Santa Claus's chair, and all the parents and children groan.

"What does it say, Raymond?" Fats asks.

"It says: 'Santa Claus Will Not be Here Today.

He Is Resting Up for Christmas. Please Come Back to See Him Tomorrow.' "

"You were right, Fats. He probably has a stomachache," I say. "He'll be back tomorrow."

But the next morning again there is no snack on my bedside table. I look out the window. The sign is still there, and Santa Claus's chair is still empty.

That does it. I decide the time has come to do a little investigating for myself.

"Gang," I announce, "I am going out there and find out what is going on."

"You can't do that, not in broad daylight with customers in the store," protests Raymond. "Adventure is adventure, Marvin, but this is too much."

"Don't worry about me," I say. Before they can stop me, I slip out the back way. I have a pretty good idea where I can find out what I want to know.

Quickly I scurry past the ranch-style dollhouse and another one with little window boxes that looks like a Swiss chalet. I drop down to the next shelf, the one where the doll beds, cradles, and high chairs are kept. Now I am right above the doll counter. Concealing myself in the bottom bunk of a double-decker doll bed, I have the perfect listening post.

The salesclerk, a red-haired woman with a figure only slightly slimmer than Santa Claus's, is just finishing a sale. As she puts a Raggedy Andy doll in a box, she is joined by the tiny gray-haired saleswoman who takes care of the stuffed animals counter.

"As I was saying, Mrs. Feldman," the large woman says, "there is something peculiar going on. It's not like Mr. Dunderhoff not to call. My land, in all the years he's been our Santa Claus, he's never missed a day."

The small woman nods. "I quite agree with you, Mrs. O'Grady. Mr. Peterson sent Joe from the stockroom over to his apartment last night, but no one was home. It certainly is odd."

A customer interrupts them, wanting to know if the store carries a doll that walks, talks, eats animal crackers, and cries real tears. But I have heard all I need to hear.

I return to our house as stealthily as I came and tell my gang what I have learned.

40

"Oh dear," cries Fats, wringing his paws. He always falls apart in a crisis.

Raymond is silent, his head buried in the morning newspaper. Suddenly he sits up straight. "Ah, here it is, just as I expected."

"What is where, just as you expected?" I demand.

Raymond peers at me over the top of his paper. "I felt sure there would be a story about Santa Claus. It's here on page sixteen."

Fats looks up. "Read it, Raymond!"

Raymond the Rat takes off his glasses. With excruciating slowness he removes a spot of imaginary dust, then puts them back on. At last he begins to read: " 'Santa Claus Missing. Beloved Macy's Santa Disappears Under Mysterious Circumstances.' That's the headline," he pauses to explain. Then he goes on:

> "One of the traditional symbols of Christmas in this city, the jovial, warm-hearted Santa Claus who has charmed thousands of young visitors to Macy's toy department for many years, disappeared mysteriously yesterday. According to spokesmen for the store, Hans Dunderhoff, who

has been Macy's Santa for eighteen years, did not report for work in the morning. Nor could he be found at his residence or at the Lexington Avenue shoe-repair shop where he works during the rest of the year. A check of area hospitals has failed to locate the 76-year-old Mr. Dunderhoff."

Raymond pauses for breath, but I notice he keeps on reading to himself.

"What else does it say?" I prod him impatiently.

"There's a lot more about how he first started playing Santa Claus," Raymond reports. "He used to dress up at Christmas to entertain his grandchildren, and when they grew up, he missed doing it. So he finally decided to close his shop for three weeks a year, telling his customers he was taking a vacation, so he could be Santa Claus for the thousands of children who visit Macy's during the Christmas season." Raymond reads some more to himself. "Fats, you'll be interested in this. It says that his beard and his stomach are real. No padding." For some reason, Fats looks proud.

"And listen to this, Marvin.

"Macy's president Frank Morgenstern attributes the store's consistently superior holiday toy sales in part to the popularity of Mr. Dunderhoff. 'We are mystified and very distressed at his disappearance,' Mr. Morgenstern told this reporter. 'He has become a traditional part of Christmas for so many New York families. Parents who remember sitting on his knee as children are now bringing their own children to the store to see him. For them, and for all our employees, it won't seem like Christmas without him.' Mr. Morgenstern asked that anyone with information about the whereabouts of Santa Claus please contact the store immediately."

Raymond puts down his newspaper. "That's the end of the story," he says. "But there's a picture of Santa Claus surrounded by children in the toy department."

Fats jumps up, knocking over his chair in his hurry to see it.

While he and Raymond study the picture, my brain is moving swiftly into action. Ever since this morning I have suspected something funny was going on, and now I am sure of it. It's not for nothing that I have led a life of crime. I know foul play when I see it.

"Gang," I say, reaching out and grabbing the newspaper to make sure I have their undivided attention, "Raymond, Fats, we must face the terrible truth. Santa Claus has been kidnaped."

5

I Become a Detective

"Have just a taste of caviar," I urge.

"No thank you, Marvin. I'm not hungry."

Who would ever have dreamed that I would be offering to share my precious jar of caviar, or that Fats would turn down flat an offer of food?

It is later that night, and besides caviar I have offered my gang an excursion to the furniture department to do acrobatic stunts on the waterbed, a Jimmy Cagney movie on the Late Show, or a game of Monopoly. Each of my ideas has been greeted with total silence.

The news that Santa Claus has been kidnaped has hit Raymond and Fats hard. Sitting at the kitchen table surrounded by food, they aren't eating a thing. They just stare morosely into space. Every once in a while Fats mumbles, "Poor Santa. Oh, what have they done to you?"

Suddenly I have had all I can take of this moping.

"Men," I say, trying to inspire them like a leader should, "sitting here feeling sorry for ourselves is not going to bring Santa Claus back. But if we snap out of it and put our brains to work, maybe we can."

I'm getting warmed up now, and I jump up on the table to make sure they take notice. "Gang," I announce, "we are going to solve this crime and get the reward."

Raymond looks up, puzzled. "What reward, Marvin?"

"It's true," I concede, "that the newspaper article didn't actually mention a reward. But there's bound to be one for the return of such a famous symbol of the Christmas spirit who has made the store piles and piles of money."

"I don't care about the reward," protests Fats. "I just want Santa Claus back. I miss him."

Raymond nods. "My feelings exactly."

No business sense, these two. All my careful training has been wasted on them.

"Are we agreed, then," I ask, "that it is up to us to rescue Santa Claus and give him back to the children of New York? After all, who is better qualified than we are to solve the case? No one knows crime like another criminal. And besides, I've always wanted to try my hand at being a detective."

"Hooray!" cries Fats. He jumps up beside me on the table and goes into the little dance he always does when he is excited, usually about cheese. "Let's go find Santa!"

"Not yet," I say, shoving him down. "First we have to plan our rescue operation."

At the word "plan" Raymond takes his pencil stub from behind his ear and gets ready to take notes. They both look at me expectantly.

There is a long silence, during which Fats helps himself generously from the caviar jar.

"Uh—Raymond," I say finally, "what do you think our first step should be?"

"The first step in solving a crime," recites Raymond like he was reading from a textbook, "is to

47

deduce the motive. Once the motive is known it should be possible to figure out who the criminal or criminals are."

"Precisely," I agree.

"What's a motive?" asks Fats.

"That's easy," I snap. "You tell him, Raymond."

"It means the reason *why* Santa Claus was kidnaped," Raymond explains.

"And the answer is obvious," I put in. "Money. Some gang knew how much Santa Claus is worth to Macy's, and they snatched him for ransom. I should have thought of the idea myself."

Raymond is busy writing something on a scrap of paper. He stops to twirl his whiskers, then writes something else.

"Don't you agree, Raymond?" I ask.

"Mmmmm, yes," he replies. "Holding him for ransom is one possibility. But—"

"But what?"

"There are other alternatives too. For example, jealousy could be a factor. Suppose some other Santa Claus was after our Santa's job. Or some other store might want him out of the way because he has helped Macy's do such a good business. Or"—Raymond looks down at his list—"it could be some very unhappy person who can't stand seeing other people feel good at Christmas time."

I consider Raymond's suggestions and quickly dismiss them. My own idea makes much more sense. After all, in the movies crimes are always committed for money. A lot of money.

"No, Raymond," I say confidently, "this job was done by professionals, I'm sure of it. Who·else could have pulled off such a smooth operation? And besides, who would want to have this fat guy on their hands unless there was a lot of money in it for them? I bet he eats a lot."

"Maybe you're right, Marvin," says Raymond, folding up his list.

"Of course I am," I say. "Now here's the plan."

Fats jumps up again, all set to rush off to the rescue.

I push him down, and this time I sit on him, just to make sure.

"We're going to do nothing," I say. "We're going to sit tight and wait for the ransom note."

49

We wait.

All the next day, and the next. Fats spends his time pacing restlessly up and down in front of the window. He walks so far I think he must have lost a whole ounce. Raymond retires to his room to read and prepare for the next phase of our rescue of Santa Claus.

I make frequent trips to my listening post, but there is no news of a ransom note.

"Jenny at the switchboard says the calls have been pouring in," Mrs. O'Grady reports. It is closing time the second day, and she is putting the dolls back in the display case. "A lot of calls are from children wanting to know if Santa Claus has been found yet. A few of them think they have seen him."

"I hear the police have been brought into the case," says Mrs. Feldman. "They are checking every lead, but the men who are supposed to look like Santa Claus are usually twenty-five years old instead of seventy-five, or they're too thin, or they have a mustache instead of a beard. All the clues so far have led to a dead end."

"Poor Mr. Dunderhoff," sighs Mrs. O'Grady. "My

land, it's quiet here without him. Mr. Peterson says business has already dropped off. I wonder if we'll ever see him again."

I don't like to admit it, but I am beginning to wonder too. I was sure a ransom note would be delivered by now. After all, as Raymond has pointed out, in order to make this caper pay off, a gang has got to move fast. "Only Nine More Shopping Days Till Christmas" reads the sign tacked up over the stuffed animals counter. Santa Claus won't be worth much ransom if he's delivered after Christmas.

I report the discouraging news to my gang.

"Maybe the ransom note got lost in the mail?" I suggest.

Raymond shakes his head. "I don't think that happens to ransom notes."

But something has happened to the ransom note. Or maybe there never was one.

That night when I suggest a raid on the delicatessen, I can hardly believe my ears. For the second time in two days I hear Fats say, "No thank you, Marvin. I'm not hungry."

52

6

I Trail a Suspect

When I awake the next morning, a strange sound greets my ears.

"Ho ho ho!" someone is saying loudly. "Merrrrrry Christmas! Ho ho ho!"

I rush to the window. A fat guy in a red suit is sitting in Santa Claus's chair. He's got a white beard and a funny-looking hat and a little kid is sitting on his knee. I reach down and pinch my tail to check if I'm still dreaming. Has our Santa Claus returned?

But then my sharp eyes notice that this fat guy's beard is on a little crooked. And his stomach isn't fat the way a true fat stomach should be—round all over like Fats's. It's only fat in one place, like maybe there's a pillow stuffed into his suit. And when he says "ho ho ho" again, there's no smile in his voice. It's fake like the rest of him. Even the little kids know it, I can tell. They're not grinning all over and giggling like they used to when Mr. Dunderhoff was here.

"He's back!" cries Fats, rudely shoving me aside so he can gawk out the window. He is bouncing up and down with such excitement that I'm afraid he's going to fall out the window again.

Raymond and I each take a leg and pull him back inside.

"He's *not* back," I tell him. "It's a new Santa Claus. Look at his phony stomach."

Fats looks, and a tear wells up in his eye and plops down on his own genuine stomach. "It's not him," he says sadly.

I return to the window to study this fake-all-over Santa Claus. I notice that he doesn't bounce babies on his knee like the real Santa Claus did. And he doesn't pat heads or let the kids tickle his stomach. He hardly even talks to them, just hands them

54

a lollipop and sends them on their way. I'm not exactly sure what this Christmas spirit is that Raymond has been talking about, but he has about as much of it as *I* do.

Suddenly something clicks in my mind.

"Raymond," I say, "I think I've got it. Remember what you said about some other Santa Claus kidnaping our Santa to get his job?"

Raymond nods.

"Well, this is the Santa Claus that did it."

Raymond considers. "He does seem somewhat lacking in the Christmas spirit," he says thoughtfully. "And I'm not sure I like the look in his eye. Maybe—"

"There's no maybe about it," I snap. "We have found the criminal."

I glance over at Fats, who is halfheartedly gnawing on a stale pretzel, the remains of the last snack Santa Claus left us before he disappeared. "Snap out of it, Fats," I say. "Tonight we rescue Santa Claus."

He pulls himself together like magic. "Hooray!" he shouts, enthusiastically bolting down the rest of the pretzel.

"Now, gang," I continue, "here is the plan.

55

When this phony Santa Claus leaves the store to-night, we follow him. He is going to lead us to *our* Santa Claus."

It is closing time. All the shoppers have gone home and the salesclerks are putting toys back in boxes and cleaning off counters. Santa Claus gets up from his chair, stretches, and waves good night to Mrs. O'Grady. Then he heads for the escalator.

This is the moment we've been waiting for.

"Let's go, men," I order, slipping out the door. I dart across the floor, Raymond and Fats close behind. I've told them this Santa Claus may move fast, and they are going to have to move just as fast to keep up with him.

I pause for a moment in the shadow of the games and puzzles counter so we can catch our breath.

Fats is already puffing and panting. A few more rescue missions like this would do wonders for his figure.

"Look, Marvin," whispers Raymond, nudging me. "He's going *up*, not down."

I look. Sure enough, a fat guy in a red suit is disappearing up the up escalator. That's strange.

"Come on, gang," I urge, yanking Fats to his feet.

Up, up, up goes Santa Claus, just like I did on the night I moved into Macy's. But when he reaches the floor with all the pianos, he gets on an elevator, me and my gang close behind.

We get off the elevator on a floor I've never seen before. There is nothing for sale up here, it's just a lot of long, bare, gray corridors and glass doors.

I look at Raymond. "Executive offices," he whispers. He points all the way down the hall to a fancy wood door with a red carpet and a huge Christmas tree in front of it. "I'll bet that is the office of Mr. Morgenstern, president of Macy's," he says.

Fats's nose twitches violently. "It's a real tree!" he exclaims. "Oh, let's just go smell it."

"No!" I hiss, grabbing him by the tail so he can't get away. Santa Claus is disappearing around the corner in the opposite direction.

"After him," I order.

We follow, but just as we turn the corner, we see him walk into an office at the end of the hall and shut the door.

Quickly I look around for a hiding place. There is no furniture in the hallway, not even a rug to slip

under. Then I spot it. Halfway down the hall is a
water fountain. The perfect listening post. I shove
Fats behind it, and Raymond follows.

Fats promptly collapses, and Raymond is breathing hard. But I am so tough I am not even winded.
After a minute I cautiously poke my head out to
size up the situation.

58

The glass door behind which Santa Claus disappeared is frosted, so we can't see what is going on inside. Above the doorknob something is written in small gold letters.

I poke Raymond the reader. "What does it say?"

He takes out his spectacles, puts them on, and squints at the sign. "It says: 'G. T. Garrity. Personnel.'"

"Of course. Uh—what's personnel?"

"That's who hired Santa Claus to work for Macy's."

Hmmmm. I wonder if this big phony actually has the nerve to ask for a raise.

From behind the door we can hear the low sound of voices. But I can't quite make out what they are saying because of the louder sound of Fats panting and wheezing next to me.

"Stop breathing," I order.

"Ho ho ho!" says one of the voices, suddenly growing louder. "All day long, it's ho ho ho, ho ho ho!" I would recognize that fake chuckle anywhere.

"I tell you, I can't take it," the voice goes on. "All that smiling and all those kids climbing on me and sticking their lollipops in my beard. I've had enough."

I look at Raymond. Somehow this conversation isn't going quite the way I expected.

"You can have this Santa Claus job," says Santa Claus. "I quit."

7

I Come Up
with a New Clue

"Only Seven More Shopping Days Till Christmas" reads the sign over the stuffed animals counter. Only seven more days, and we haven't got a single clue.

All the next day Raymond and Fats mope around the house with long faces. It's depressing. By closing time I can't stand it.

"Let's go raid the delicatessen," I suggest.

Fats doesn't even look up.

"A watermelon pickle will cheer you up," I assure him.

He still doesn't budge.

"Have you ever tried a peanut butter and watermelon-pickle sandwich?" I ask him. "I hear it's delicious."

In spite of himself he starts to look interested.

"Come on, gang," I say. "Let's eat."

Two hours later we are lounging on a velvet pillow in front of a color set in the TV department, our stomachs full to the brim, our troubles almost forgotten. We're in luck—one of our favorite old gangster movies is playing on the Late Show, and Fats is in seventh heaven. Waving the last of his peanut butter and watermelon-pickle sandwich, he cheers on the bad guys as they prepare to blast their way into the bank vault.

I have seen this movie about twelve times, so I'm not giving it my full attention. With the taste of caviar lingering in my mouth and the soft velvet under my head, I doze off.

"Oh, rats!" cries Fats, stamping his foot.

That means the good guys have triumphed again. I open my eyes to see the cops snapping handcuffs on the bank robbers. The newspaper reporter is saying to the police chief, "I'll tell you how I knew it

was Freddy the Fox and his gang. The criminal always returns to the scene of the crime."

I yawn and stretch. The movie is over. Time for bed.

"That's it!" says Raymond. He is sitting up straight, staring at the TV set with a strange little smile on his face. "Marvin, I think I've got it."

"Got what?" I ask lazily.

"A clue to who kidnaped Santa Claus."

I wake up fast, and even Fats stops shaking his fist at the TV screen and pays attention.

"I got the idea from the last scene in the movie," Raymond starts to explain. "You know, when the reporter turns to the police chief and says, 'The criminal always returns to the scene of the crime.' "

"Yes, yes," I snap impatiently. "What's the clue?"

"I'm coming to that," Raymond answers. He can't be hurried. He has to think things through. Sometimes I think I should have named him Raymond the Turtle instead of Raymond the Rat.

"It reminded me of a customer I have observed whose behavior seems suspicious," Raymond goes on. "He is a thin man about medium height, and he wears a gray overcoat and hat. He comes in almost every day at the same time—right after lunch—and he doesn't buy anything. He just kind of stands around the games and puzzles counter."

"What's so suspicious about that?" I scoff. "Maybe he's too poor to buy, but he likes to look. Lots of people do."

"That's not all," Raymond continues as if I hadn't interrupted. "He gets into the line with all the par-

I Come Up with a New Clue

ents and children waiting to see Santa Claus. But he doesn't have a child with him."

"Hmmmm," I say. This is a little unusual, I have to admit. Still, it could be that this guy is hungry and wants a lollipop for lunch. After all, why should kids be the only ones to get the free handouts?

"He never stays until he gets to the front of the line, though," Raymond says. "Just when he's almost there, he suddenly looks at his watch and hurries away."

"Mmm-*hmmmm*," I say. Maybe Raymond has got something at that. It is worth investigating anyway. I know from watching a lot of detective movies that it's often the smallest clue that breaks the case wide open. And besides, we don't have any other clues.

"All right, Raymond," I say. "When the store opens on Monday, we look for this lurker."

"And then we follow him and find Santa Claus and rescue him," adds Fats excitedly. "Hooray!"

"No," I say firmly.

He looks surprised.

"You heard Raymond say he was a skinny guy," I say. "Skinny guys move fast, and this time we can't take a chance on losing him. No, gang, this is a one-man mission. It calls for someone tough and fast and slippery. Someone who knows his way around and won't lose his head. Someone who can stick to this lurker like a shadow. Namely me."

8

I Undertake
a Dangerous Mission

So again we wait. I never knew before that being a detective was all waiting around for something to happen. My feet are itching for action.

I am sprawled out on my bed munching on sunflower seeds from a bag that Fats lifted from the health-food counter last night. According to him, they are packed full of vitamins and are guaranteed to give me the quick energy I need for the dangerous mission ahead. They must be packed full of something because it sure isn't flavor.

Fats and Raymond are keeping watch at my two

windows. It's almost lunchtime, and so far no lurker has shown up. Not many children have either. Mrs. O'Grady was right: without Mr. Dunderhoff, business is definitely off. Today no one is sitting in Santa Claus's big chair.

"These sunflower seeds taste like pigeon food," I complain. "Is all health food this bad?"

Fats nods sadly. "That's how you know it's good for you."

I spit them out and reach for a hunk of Coon cheddar that I have tucked away under my pillow. I figure I have all the quick energy I need anyway.

Suddenly I notice Fats is jumping up and down at the window. "It's him!" he sputters. "He's back!"

I leap from my bed and shove him aside so I can see. "Where?" I demand. I don't see any skinny guy in a gray overcoat.

Fats points. "Not the lurker," he says, a big idiotic grin on his face. "Santa Claus!"

I look. Sure enough, there is a fat guy in a red suit sitting in Santa Claus's chair. But this time I can tell at a glance it's not our Santa Claus. All of him looks real, all right, but his cheeks aren't rosy enough and his stomach isn't fat enough. And instead of a long white beard he has a straggly blond one. This Santa is just a boy.

Fats is watching me closely. "Is it—"

"No." I shake my head. "It's not him."

I check this new Santa Claus over carefully for a few minutes. He's not as bad as the last one, I decide. He bounces the kids on his knee and talks with them, at least. But he's not Mr. Dunderhoff. His "ho ho ho"'s sound more like "har de harr har"'s. And instead of patting the kids on the head and saying "Merry Christmas," he kind of pokes them in the ribs and says, "Have a cool Yule, man."

He will never do, I tell myself.

Just then Raymond says, "Marvin, it's him."

"No it isn't," I tell him. "It's just another phony."

"I mean the lurker. He's at the puzzle counter."

I race to the other window, shoving Raymond aside. At first glance I don't see any lurker. But finally I locate a skinny guy in a gray overcoat standing at the games and puzzles counter looking over a stack of jigsaw puzzles. He doesn't look suspicious to me. In fact, he looks so ordinary I bet his own mother couldn't pick him out of a crowd. But then I tell myself that in the movies it's always the guy who looks the most innocent who turns out to be the master criminal.

Raymond edges in beside me, and we watch the suspect as he lurks around the puzzle counter for a few minutes, then joins the growing line of kids and parents waiting to see Santa Claus.

A few more minutes go by, and he's third in line after a lady with twins and a man carrying a baby in a pink snowsuit.

"Get ready, Marvin," warns Raymond.

"Good luck," whispers Fats, shoving a handful of sunflower seeds at me.

"Don't worry about Marvin the Magnificent," I say. "I'm tough and I'm fast and I'm slippery."

I hurry downstairs and wait by our front door, peering out the mail slot. Just like Raymond said, as the lady with twins plops them on Santa Claus's lap, the lurker looks at his watch. Then he puts on his hat, pulls up the collar of his coat, and walks away.

I'm out the door and after him like greased lightning. I know if I don't catch up with him right away, I'll lose him forever.

By the time he steps onto the down escalator, I am right beside him, standing close—but not too close —to his black oxfords. Down we go, and I'm stuck to him like glue, keeping one eye out for old women with seven shopping bags and other dangerous types. So far so good. But I know the real test will come when we leave the store. If I lose him for a second, I'm finished. A guy in a gray overcoat with black oxfords will be swallowed up in the crowd as soon as he hits the street.

I sneak a peek up at him and notice that the gray overcoat has a large pocket. For a moment I'm tempted to hop in and hitch a ride. But I know from experience that this could be a trap, one from which I might not escape alive. So instead I do something so clever even Raymond would never have thought of it.

Resting on the step in front of me is a large red package decorated with little red-and-white stickers with Santa Claus's face on them. I reach out and peel one off. Then I step around behind the suspect and carefully attach the sticker to his right shoe just above the sole. Now his black oxfords are different from all

72

other black oxfords in the crowd. All I have to do is follow the Santa Claus face, and he can't give me the slip.

It works perfectly. We step off the escalator onto the main floor, and I have no trouble staying with the suspect as he walks through the revolving door to the street, then stops for a red light. Across the street a lot of people have stopped to listen to a brass band playing Christmas carols. But my man doesn't seem to have the Christmas spirit—he hurries past and down the block. It's hard keeping up with him, but I catch him when he has to stop for another light.

I'm just beginning to wonder how far this mission is going to take me and whether I'll be able to find my way back when suddenly the suspect makes a right turn into a revolving door. Quickly I lunge for the next compartment. I make it, but the door spins violently, and I am thrown to the floor. When I open my eyes, I find myself lying in a heap inside a store. I blink. It looks just like Macy's, but it can't be. Then I remember: Macy's biggest rival is just a block away. This must be Gimbels. I pick myself up just in time to see that little Santa Claus face winking at me as the black oxfords disappear into the distance.

I can't let him get away now. Pulling myself together, I'm after him again, darting through a forest of pant legs and high-heeled shoes. Luckily the crowd slows him down too, and I catch my man just as he steps onto the up escalator.

I have a minute to rest and congratulate myself on the brilliant way I have handled this difficult mission. Then the suspect is stepping off the escalator. I'm close behind as he walks quickly through the record department and the book department. Suddenly I'm in a place that looks strangely familiar. There are piles of jigsaw puzzles, towers of blocks, shelves of stuffed animals and dolls, fleets of trucks exactly my size, an electric train. The music is even the same. That song about the reindeer with a light bulb for a nose is really starting to get on my nerves. Gimbels has a toy department just like Macy's.

I can't resist pausing for a moment to gaze up at the electric train. It's bigger and shinier than the one

74

at Macy's, and it looks like it might go even faster. If only I had time to take a ride. It's only for an instant that I contemplate the idea. But when I look around, the suspect is disappearing through a door at the back of the toy department. I'm after him like a shot, but just as I reach the door, it slams shut, nearly shaving off my whiskers.

"Rats!" I mutter. After sticking to him like a shadow through revolving doors, escalators, and city streets, I've lost him after all.

I step back to survey the barrier that stands between me and the suspect. I notice that halfway up, printed in black letters, there is a sign. My reading isn't as good as Raymond's, but I've seen this sign before in the movie theater and I know that it says "Employees Only." The door itself is constructed of metal, too heavy to push open. And there is no crack wide enough for me to slip under. But what goes in must come out, I figure. So, making myself as comfortable as possible behind a trash barrel, I settle down to wait.

For many minutes I wait. No one comes out. No one goes in. I am beginning to think that door has swallowed our suspect alive, and he will never be seen again.

And then the door opens. But it isn't the skinny guy in the gray overcoat who comes out. It is Santa Claus.

9

I Plan a Rescue Operation

"Did you find him? Did you find him?" Fats asks eagerly, bouncing up and down on my bed like a yo-yo.

Raymond looks up expectantly from the paperback book he is reading in my rocking chair.

There is no use beating around the bush. It is embarrassing for a leader to have to admit defeat, but I might as well tell them. "No," I say. "The suspect escaped."

Fats collapses on my pillow, a limp bundle of fat misery. Raymond closes his book. I notice from the cover that it's a detective story. One thing you have to say about Raymond, he does his homework.

"Where did you lose him?" he asks quietly.

I tell them the whole story, starting with my flawless tailing of the suspect and my brilliant ploy with the Santa Claus sticker and ending with the mysterious door that swallowed up the suspect.

"And after Santa Claus came out," I say in conclusion,. "I waited some more. I watched that door like a hawk for an hour. But no one else came out."

I wait for Raymond to say something, but he is silent. I glance over at the bed. Fats is drowning his sorrows in chocolate-covered marshmallow cookies and has completely disappeared inside the box. There is no sound except for muffled lip-smacking and the squeak of my rocking chair going back and forth, back and forth. Raymond has taken off his glasses and is absentmindedly chewing on one of the stems as he rocks. I recognize the signs, and I am quiet. Raymond the Rat is thinking.

After a couple of minutes the squeaking stops. Raymond clears his throat. "Marvin," he says, "there is only one possible explanation. You did not lose the suspect."

"I didn't?" I feel better already.

"No. All we have to do is look at the situation logically, and we can deduce what happened. First of all, we know it isn't possible for the suspect to have been magically swallowed up when he went through that door. And from my experience with employees' lounges, it seems unlikely that it has another exit through which he could have escaped. Therefore he must have come out."

"I told you," I say irritably, "I didn't close my eyes for a second. And the only person who came out was Gimbels' Santa Claus."

"Exactly."

He can't mean what I think he means. Raymond has gone too far this time. "You mean you think that skinny guy took off his overcoat and turned himself into Santa Claus in the men's room?"

"Absolutely. All it takes is a few pillows, a fake white beard, and a Santa Claus suit."

He does mean what I think he means. "Then the lurker is really the Gimbels Santa Claus in disguise?"

"Precisely. And it is a very clever disguise. All he has to do is take off his Santa Claus costume and put on his regular clothes, and no one will ever recognize him."

I think this over carefully, and my sharp brain comes to a swift conclusion. "Raymond," I say, "this is definitely suspicious."

Raymond nods solemnly. "I think we have found our man."

Fats suddenly pops out of the cookie box. With chocolate in his fur and crumbs in his whiskers, he looks like a chocolate-covered marshmallow cookie himself. "What man?" he demands. "Where is he? Has he got Santa Claus?"

Raymond explains his theory all over again, then adds, "The motive for the crime must have been jealousy, just as I suspected. It's only natural that with Macy's Santa Claus so popular the Santa Clauses in other stores would feel bad. Probably the Gimbels Santa just couldn't take it anymore. He may have thought that if he could get this famous Macy's Santa out of the way, more children would come to see *him*."

It does make a certain amount of sense, I have to admit. But right now I am not interested in explanations. What we need is action.

"Gang," I announce, "I am going after this villain in a Santa Claus suit again, and this time I'm going to stick to him until he leads me to the real Santa Claus."

Fats slides off the bed and stands in front of me, trying very hard to suck in his stomach. "Can I go this time?" he asks hopefully. "I'm tough and I'm fast and I'm slippery."

I pace the floor, considering. As I pass the window, I glance outside. The sign over the stuffed animals counter catches my eye. "Only Six More Shopping Days Till Christmas," it says.

My mind is made up.

"Here is the plan, gang," I tell them. "This time we're all going, and we're not coming back without Santa Claus."

Raymond nods thoughtfully. "We'll need certain equipment," he says, "for the rescue operation."

"Of course," I agree.

"I think I have it all on hand," he says. "Follow me."

We all go into Raymond's room. Since Raymond moved in, it has gotten so crowded that it looks like a second-hand store. Piled from floor to ceiling is a leaning tower of unmatched mittens. Other things he has scavenged recently are stacked all around: baseball cards, four dominos, a comic book, assorted doll clothes, bubble gum, several toy wristwatches, some play money, a rubber duck, three pacifiers, and a complete collection of spare parts for toy cars.

Raymond immediately disappears into his bottom drawer. For several minutes dust and strange objects fly through the air, but no Raymond emerges.

While we are waiting, I decide to give Fats a quick course in body-building.

"Lie flat on the floor," I instruct. "Now push your whole body off the floor with your arms."

But though he struggles for several minutes, he can't get that king-sized stomach off the floor.

"That's enough push-ups," I say. "Let's try some boxing."

I hold out a pillow from Raymond's bed for a punching bag. Fats takes a tremendous wind-up, misses the pillow completely, and sprawls flat on his nose.

He is a hopeless case.

"On second thought," I tell him, "maybe you better just rest."

There is a big commotion in the bottom drawer, and Raymond steps out holding up several objects in triumph. "I think I've located everything we'll need," he says. "If you'll just hold this mitten, Marvin, I'll pack it up."

I hold open a navy-blue mitten, and Raymond drops in these items one by one:

A key ring with about fourteen keys. ("For opening doors, of course," says Raymond. "It has taken me a lifetime to collect this many keys.")

A ball of heavy string. ("For scaling walls and lassoing things.")

A Boy Scout pocket knife. ("To help us get in and out of places. It has three different blades plus a nail file and a can opener.")

A tiny notebook with a pencil attached. ("For taking notes, drawing maps, and leaving messages.")

A little leather bag full of marbles. ("Our secret weapon in case we are trapped. We throw them on the floor, our enemy trips, and we make our getaway.")

And finally, a large, tattered man's handkerchief with the initial *G* in the corner. ("That's our disguise.")

"Disguise?" I repeat. "What kind of dumb disguise is that?" I prefer my rubber nose, fake mustache, and sunglasses.

"It's the perfect portable disguise for the three of us," Raymond explains. "If we get into a tight spot and can't find a hiding place, we simply throw this over us, and we look like an old rag someone has thrown away."

It's so simple it just might work at that.

Just before Raymond closes up the mitten, Fats drops in a little package wrapped up in a Snickers wrapper.

"What's that?" I demand.

"Emergency rations," he replies. "A hunk of Wisconsin cheddar, to keep our strength up."

Raymond ties the mitten shut with a shoelace.

"All right, men," I say. "Everything is ready for our rescue operation. This mission is going to call for all our strength and speed and cunning. So sleep well, gang. At dawn we're off to rescue Santa Claus."

10

I Find Santa Claus

"Who would ever have thought it," sighs Fats with a foolish grin. "A real castle just our size."

It sits up high and safe on a shelf like our house at Macy's, and it's just like the castles we've seen in the movies, complete with a moat and a drawbridge, turrets and a look-out tower. When I spotted it yesterday during my long wait in Gimbels' toy department, I knew it would be the perfect hiding place.

"Don't just stand there gawking," I order. "Up and inside."

We scurry to the top shelf, step across the drawbridge, and we're inside our own little castle.

In the courtyard there are little plastic knights all dressed in armor, their swords ready to attack.

"I've always wanted to fight a dragon," cries Fats, grabbing a loose sword and swinging it through the air. He narrowly misses removing Raymond's head. "Take that!"

We quickly disarm him and drag him into the lookout tower. It is from here that we will keep watch over the Gimbels Santa Claus until the store closes. Then, after he leads us to where he has hidden our Santa Claus, we will perform the great rescue.

Raymond stations himself at one of the slits in the wall that serve as peepholes while Fats curls up to rest. In a moment he is snoring.

"I can see the suspect," Raymond reports. "He has a little girl on his knee."

All afternoon Raymond and I take turns watching. It is a very long afternoon. Santa Claus sits on a platform surrounded by giant candy canes. Dozens of kids climb up on his knee, say a few words, and are handed a balloon with a reindeer on it. There are about as many kids here as at Macy's, Raymond estimates, but not as many as used to come to see Mr. Dunderhoff. I have plenty of time to study this Santa Claus and compare him with the others I've met recently. I don't like what I see. This one doesn't have phony "ho ho ho"s—he doesn't laugh at all. He doesn't even smile. And since he doesn't smile at the kids, they don't smile either. This toy department is a glum place. I'm beginning to understand now why Mr. Dunderhoff was so popular. I even think I have an idea what the Christmas spirit is all about. It's got something to do with smiling, and it seems to be catching, like a cold in the nose.

Promptly at dinnertime Fats wakes up and starts complaining about how hungry he is.

"Tough guys don't whine," I tell him sternly.

"How can I be tough when I'm weak with hunger?" he whines.

I can see there is only one way to keep him quiet, so I bring out the cheese. After dinner Fats takes a turn at the peephole while Raymond checks over his equipment and I take a short nap.

"He's leaving!" shouts Fats suddenly. I rush to the window just in time to see Santa Claus's red hat passing right below us.

"This is it, men," I say. "After him!"

We're over the castle wall and hit the floor running, past the electric train, past the towers of blocks, and out of the toy department. I spot him ahead of us in the record department, and we catch up when he stops to wait for the elevator. We wait too. When it comes, we step to the rear of the car. Then it's down to the main floor, out through a back door that must be for employees only, and we're on the street.

The night is cold, and the smell of snow is in the air, just like the night when I first came to Macy's. But the streets are bustling with lights, horns blaring, people hurrying home with their arms full of packages. From the next corner I can faintly hear Christmas carols being played by a brass band. For some reason, the sound warms me up.

"All right, gang," I hiss. "Let's go."

But Fats is standing perfectly still staring up into the sky with his mouth hanging open. "It must be the biggest, most beautiful tree in the whole world," he whispers, his voice full of awe.

I follow his gaze. There in the middle of all the traffic is a giant Christmas tree covered with red and white lights. On its topmost branch, halfway up into the sky, gleams a yellow star.

It's big all right. And that star seems to beckon us on as it sways in the wind.

But this is no time to be mooning over Christmas trees. "Let's go," I order again, giving Fats's ear a sharp pinch of encouragement. "Remember, if we lose our man now, we've lost Santa Claus forever."

This gets him moving at last. And luck is with us: our suspect seems to be in no hurry. I soon find out, too, that a man in a red suit stands out in any crowd. We have no trouble keeping up with him as he walks a block, crosses the street, then goes down the steps to the subway.

It is then that something strange happens. I take my eye off him for a moment while I'm squeezing Fats through the bars of the exit gate, and when I look up, there are two Santa Clauses.

One is about to sit down on a bench, and the other is walking away down the platform.

"It's this one!" cries Fats, tugging at my arm and pointing down the platform.

I look. But right away I know he is the wrong one. He is smiling.

90

Quickly I check the Santa who is sitting on the bench. His face is glum.

Like a true leader, I make a swift, sure decision. "Men," I say, "this is the Santa we are after."

We duck under the bench he's sitting on to wait for the train. When it comes, we use the tactic I've devised for rush-hour travel, waiting until all the people are inside and the doors are closing before we hop on board. Again we station ourselves under the seat, close to Santa Claus's feet. We ride for a long time, long enough for Fats to check out all the candy wrappers under the seat and report with a plainly broken heart that no one has discarded any candy. Raymond digs out his notebook and starts drawing a little map of where we are, so we'll be able to get back.

He peers out at the sign on the wall as the train comes into another station. "King's Highway," he reports. "I think we're in Brooklyn."

I look out to see if the station looks any different. I've never been in Brooklyn before.

Just then I notice that Santa Claus is standing up. "Get ready for action, gang," I warn. We are close at his heels as he steps off the train, pushes through the exit door, and climbs the stairs to the street.

A gust of cold air greets us as we step outside. Looking up at the street light, I can see snowflakes swirling in the wind, and I shiver. Our man must feel it through his Santa Claus suit because he walks faster now, down a wide street filled with shops and bright lights. We pass another Santa Claus ringing a bell on a corner, and our suspect waves to him.

The snow is starting to stick to the pavement, and Fats is whining that his feet are cold. "Can't we stop and rest for a minute?" he pleads. But I have no mercy. I drag him along by the ear.

Ahead of us the suspect suddenly stops and goes inside a little store on the corner. As Fats collapses gratefully in a heap and Raymond whips out his notebook, I press my nose against the glass.

"It's a delicatessen," Raymond informs me, scribbling away like mad.

"I know that," I snap. I've spent enough time in delicatessens to know one when I smell one.

"He's ordering a sandwich and coffee to take out," Raymond reports. "No, two coffees and two sandwiches. Corned beef on rye, I think. With pickles."

At the sound of the magic word, Fats comes suddenly to life. He drags himself to his feet, ready to follow a pickle to the ends of the earth.

The door opens, and out comes our suspect carrying a small brown bag. We follow him as he turns the corner onto a side street. This street is dimly lit and lined with rundown-looking buildings. He climbs the steps of a brownstone apartment house and unlocks the front door.

"Quick, after him!" I shout.

We barely make it through the door before it slams. Looking up, I can see a pair of legs in a red suit disappearing up a steep staircase. Raymond and I push Fats, huffing and puffing, to the top. But when we get there, those Santa Claus legs are just vanishing up another flight.

Fats takes one look at the stairs and refuses to budge. "I can't go another step," he wheezes.

"Nonsense!" I snap. "Tough guys never give up."

"Fats," Raymond says quietly. "You know who is at the top of these stairs, don't you? It's Santa Claus. *Our* Santa Claus."

By superhuman effort, Fats manages to crawl up

the last flight. Now we can hear footsteps at the end of a dark hallway. There is the sound of a door closing and locks clicking. Cautiously we tiptoe down the hall and stop in front of the last door.

"Ssssh!" I whisper. We listen.

For a moment we hear nothing. Then, very softly, the sound of two voices.

"Please," one is saying, "release me now. I promise I will not go the police. I will say nothing to anyone."

"It's him!" squeals Fats. "It's ——!"

I clap my paw over his mouth, but I'm feeling as excited as he is. At last we've found Santa Claus.

"Relax," a low voice replies. "There's only five more days before Christmas, and then I'll be catching a plane for Florida, and you'll be free to go back to your shoe shop. Think of this as a vacation. The accommodations may not be deluxe, but you got nothing to do all day but rest."

"I've had too much rest," says Mr. Dunderhoff. "I am not used to it. I like to be busy. And I miss the children."

"Well, I can tell you I'm not going to miss those little creeps when I'm lying in the sun down south.

After a day of them crawling all over me and then slogging home through the snow, I can use some rest. I'm going to turn in."

"I'll just listen to the radio for a little while," says Mr. Dunderhoff. "I always like to hear the evening symphony."

There are sounds of chairs scraping the floor, shoes dropping, water running, and then silence except for the occasional high thin squeak of violins.

Raymond and I look at each other. Now, while the villain sleeps, is our chance to rescue Santa Claus. But how?

"We're coming, Santa," Fats whispers reassuringly. "Hang on."

Raymond has stepped back to look over the door. I note that it is made of wood and painted a faded pea-green, with black letters identifying it as "3D." But Raymond isn't looking at that. He is studying the locks.

There are three of them, one under the doorknob and two right above. Raymond reaches into his mitten, rummages around, and comes out with his key ring. "I knew these would come in handy someday," he says, looking pleased.

Of course. This operation is child's play. And I, Marvin the Magnificent, will perform the heroic rescue.

"Good work, Raymond," I say. "Now, if you'll just assist me with the rope, I'll have Santa Claus out of there in no time at all."

Raymond hands me the coil of string, and I make a loop in the end for a lasso. I swing it around my head a few times like they do in the movies, then let it fly. It's as good a throw as a real cowboy could make, but it falls a little short. After all, a doorknob is a lot smaller than a cow. But after a few more tries, the loop settles beautifully over the doorknob, and I pull it tight. Handing Raymond the end of the rope and taking the key ring in my teeth, I shinny up the rope just like Tarzan of the apes.

In a moment I am standing on the doorknob waving triumphantly to Raymond and Fats. It occurs to me then that they look very far away, and the doorknob is a little bit slippery. I decide not to look down again. I get right to work, trying the first key in the top lock as quietly as a burglar. It won't go in, so I try the next. I try nearly every key on that key ring before one goes in. At last we've got it!

97

But the key refuses to turn. I try to remove it, but it won't come out either. Impatiently I tug at the key, and suddenly it does come out, catching me off-balance. For a moment I teeter on that doorknob like a circus performer doing a high-wire act. Then I plunge to the floor.

Luckily I land on something soft, something that breaks my fall like a fat, fluffy pillow. I open my eyes. What I've landed on is Fats.

Raymond is hovering over us, saying, "Oh dear, are you all right?"

I nod. "That was quick thinking, Fats," I say.

But he doesn't answer. His eyes are closed, and he looks like a doormat. Raymond shakes him. "Fats, wake up! Oh, if only I'd brought the smelling salts."

Finally he opens his eyes. "Where am I?" he asks weakly. "What happened?"

After Raymond explains how he saved my life, Fats recovers rapidly. "I did that?" he says. "How brave!"

I'm all ready to climb up the rope again when Raymond says, "It's no use, Marvin. We don't have

98

the right keys. Even if you could open one of the locks, you could never do all three."

I have the feeling he is right. I step back to look over the door again. But what I'm looking for isn't there. There are no chinks or cracks that we could enlarge to mouse size like we did at the cheese store. With his appetite, Fats could probably eat through the entire door, but that would take too long. Time is running out.

"Gang," I say, "there is only one thing to do. We have found out where Santa Claus is. Now we must come up with a bold new plan to save him. We will retreat tonight, but tomorrow we shall return."

Raymond nods in agreement. He makes a few notes in his notebook. Then he tears off a little scrap of paper, writes something on it, and carefully wraps it up in the Snickers wrapper Fats brought along.

"What are you doing?" I demand.

"Leaving Santa Claus a message," he explains. "When he sees the Snickers wrapper, he'll know who it is from, and it will give him hope."

"What does it say?" I ask.

" '*Courage*,' " replies Raymond.

11

I Lead an Ambush

"Can we blast?" Fats asks hopefully.

We are sitting around our kitchen table the next morning nibbling on cereal and sunflower seeds—all that is left in our larder—and trying to come up with a bold new rescue plan.

I consider Fats's idea. This is the way the bank robbers always break into the vault in the movies, but it's noisy and messy, and they always get caught in the end. I have a better idea.

"The thing to do," I tell my gang, "is capture the suspect and torture him into confessing." I've seen

100

this done a lot in foreign spy movies.

"Oh, goodie!" cheers Fats.

I look at Raymond. He is chewing on a sunflower seed and staring into space. "Well," I say, "what do you think of my plan?"

Raymond pushes his glasses down to the end of his nose and peers over them at me. "I think," he says slowly, "that you are forgetting one thing. This enemy outweighs us, and he can easily outrun us as well. What we need is a plan to outwit him using our brains instead of our muscles."

I flex my biceps. There's nothing wrong with my muscles. They are as hard as nails. Still, Raymond has a point. Our size is a handicap in dealing with someone as big as this Santa Claus. My razor-sharp brain, on the other hand, is my most powerful weapon.

Reaching into the box on the table, I stuff a handful of cereal into my mouth. "Yuck!" I spit it out. "What is this stuff anyway?"

"It's crunchy granola," says Fats. "It's very good for you."

I might have known. What it needs is a little caviar to perk it up. I check the cupboard and find, way in back, a caviar jar with a few spoonfuls left that I saved for a rainy day. If ever I needed it, I need it now. I spread some on the granola and pop it into my mouth.

"Mmmm," I say. "That's better."

It is then, while I am chewing, that I have my great idea. I've heard fish is good for the brain, but I never knew it worked this fast.

"I've got it," I announce. "A plan that is bold, foolproof, and uses our brains instead of our muscles."

They are all ears.

"My plan is simple and beautiful," I tell them. "You know the table with all the trains and planes and other battery toys?" Raymond nods. "Well, we borrow a few of them and then we sit back and wait for our suspect to pay his daily visit to Macy's. It's an ambush, like in the war movies. When he shows up, we release the toys, tripping the suspect."

"Hooray!" shouts Fats, clapping his paws in delight.

"That's not all," I go on. "Now comes the good part. While he is on the floor, we pick his pockets, steal his keys, and quick as a flash we're off to rescue Santa Claus."

Fats is so excited he hops up on the table and starts doing his famous cheese dance.

"It was nothing, really," I say modestly. "Just a brilliant idea I had."

But Raymond is shaking his head worriedly. "I don't know, Marvin. It's risky. What if he doesn't fall? Or what if we can't find the keys? I've never picked a pocket before."

"Well, I have," I assure him. "There's nothing to it. We each take a pocket, and it's in and out before he knows what hit him."

Raymond still looks dubious, but I say, "Courage. We can't fail. Come on, there are only a few minutes left before the store opens. Just enough time to prepare our trap."

"Weapons ready?" I whisper to my men.

They nod. We are concealed beneath the bottom branches of a large Christmas tree that is strategically located between the puzzle counter and the entrance to the line for Santa Claus. We have bor-

103

rowed a whole fleet of battery toys: a train, a motor-cycle, a police car, a dune buggy, a robot, a clown that beats on a drum, a cat that rolls over, and—the final touch—a mouse.

"What time is it?" I ask, giving Raymond the elbow. It's getting hot in here, and I get stuck with plastic pine needles every time I move.

Raymond creeps over to the other side of the tree where he has a good view of the cuckoo clock on the wall. He comes back to report, "It's ten of one. Almost time."

Fats takes a deep breath, then wrinkles up his nose in disgust. "The Christmas tree we had in the cheese store last year had a delicious smell, like fresh air. This one smells like mothballs."

"Never mind that," I say, giving him my other elbow. "On your feet and ready for action."

While Raymond keeps watch on the puzzle counter, Fats and I line up our weapons and point them in the right direction. We check to make sure they are all working properly. Everything is ready for the attack.

"Black shoes stopping at the puzzle counter," announces Raymond. I take a deep breath. "No—false alarm. Too big."

Then a minute later: "Another pair of black shoes approaching. Hold on—yes, the right one has a peeling-off Santa Claus sticker. It's our suspect."

Fats and I stand at attention, our paws poised on the release buttons.

"He's still standing there," reports Raymond. "Probably pretending to look at puzzles while he counts up how many customers the toy department has today."

I make a last-minute adjustment on the robot.

"Now he's moving away from the counter," Raymond says. "He's coming this way. Get ready—aim —fire!"

We unleash our weapons, then stand back to watch the results.

Our aim is deadly. First, the motorcycle darts in front of the suspect, causing him to stumble. Then the cat rolling in circles around his left leg knocks him off balance. As he flails his arms wildly, struggling to stay on his feet, the dune buggy brings him down with a crash.

105

My plan is working perfectly. "Ready for Step Two," I whisper. "Remember, in and out of those pockets like lightning."

But then something happens that I hadn't figured on. The mouse has crossed the path of a tall woman with three shopping bags. She shrieks and falls on top of the suspect, scattering packages everywhere. Two old ladies in fur coats stumble over the packages and go down screaming. A salesman from the puzzle counter comes rushing to the rescue, but he is ambushed by the police car and takes a nosedive. More shoppers coming to see what is going on end up on the floor, putting the entire toy department in an uproar.

"Oh no!" I groan. My plan has worked too perfectly. Not only have we trapped our suspect but dozens of innocent bystanders as well.

As we stand by watching helplessly, we see our suspect struggle to his feet, mumble an apology to the woman with the shopping bags, dust himself off, and quietly make his escape.

"What do we do now?" wails Fats with tears in his eyes.

"Rats!" I mutter. "Foiled again."

12

I Devise a Bold, Foolproof New Plan

"Macy's Santa Claus still missing," says Raymond. He is rocking and thinking in my rocking chair late that night.

"You don't have to rub it in," I mumble through a mouthful of caviar. Fats and I have just returned from a raid on the delicatessen during which I recklessly lifted three jars of it. I figure if I stuff myself with brain food, another brilliant idea will be bound to strike me.

"I'm not rubbing it in," answers Raymond. "I'm reading this afternoon's paper."

108

I drop my caviar, Fats abandons a box of animal crackers, and we peer over Raymond's shoulder.

"There's no picture," laments Fats right away.

"It's a shorter article this time," adds Raymond.

"Read it," I order.

Raymond adjusts his spectacles and begins:

> "There is a little less joy in Christmas this year for thousands of children in the New York area. With the holiday only four days away, there is still no trace of their favorite symbol of Christmas, Macy's Santa Claus, who disappeared on December 12. Hans Dunderhoff, who was the department store's Santa for eighteen years, brought an extra measure of Christmas spirit to his job, bringing children and their parents back to see him year after year."

There it is again, that Christmas spirit.

> "Police, working closely with Macy's officials, have followed up more than fifty tips, many of them from children who telephoned the store to report that they had seen Mr. Dunderhoff. But so far all leads have failed to turn up the missing Santa Claus.
>
> "According to Kenneth Peterson, manager of

Macy's toy department, toy sales have been disappointing since the disappearance of Mr. Dunderhoff. But most disappointed of all are the children. They still come to Macy's each day, their faces aglow with the anticipation of seeing their favorite Father Christmas. They leave looking strangely subdued. With their Santa Claus missing, some of the joy of the holiday season is missing too."

There is a long silence.

"Poor children," says Raymond softly. I think I detect a wetness in his eyes fogging up his glasses.

"Poor us," sniffs Fats. Two gigantic tears roll down his face and plop onto the newspaper.

I can see that it is up to me, as usual, to snap them out of it.

"Garbage!" I snort, which makes them take notice. "If we sit around crying we'll never rescue Santa Claus and become heroes and get the reward. All is not lost. *We* know where Santa Claus is. We just have to let the rest of the world know."

A strange expression crosses Raymond's face. "Marvin," he says wonderingly. "You've got it!"

"Got what?"

110

"The best idea yet. It's bold, it's foolproof, and it uses our brains instead of our muscles." Raymond looks relieved, as if our rescue has already been accomplished. Fats jumps up and slaps me on the back. "Congratulations!" he cries. Reaching into the cracker box, he swallows a hippopotamus and an elephant one after the other.

"It was nothing," I tell him. "Uh—Raymond— what's my idea?"

But Raymond has already left the rocking chair and is on his way out the door. I follow him across the hall to his room, Fats close behind. We watch as he opens and closes drawers, assembling a pile of objects in the middle of the floor.

"There," he says at last, sitting down next to a stack of newspapers and comic books. "I think that's everything we need."

"Need for what?" I ask.

"For the letter, of course," he says. He takes a pencil stub from behind his ear and starts scribbling in his notebook.

After a minute he pauses, crosses something out, and twirls his whiskers furiously. As usual when Raymond is thinking, Fats and I keep silent. It is so quiet you can hear Fats's cookie crumbs dropping.

"How's this?" he says finally, ripping a page out of his notebook. " 'Dear Mr. Harry Walker: We have discovered the whereabouts of Macy's Santa Claus. He is being held against his will at the below address. Please ask the police to act quickly to return Santa Claus to the children of New York in time for Christmas.' "

Raymond looks at me over his glasses. "Well?"

"It's a fine letter," I tell him. "There is only one thing I don't quite understand. Who is Mr. Harry Walker?"

"The reporter," replies Raymond. "The one who wrote the two stories in the *New York Globe*."

Now at last my idea is clear to me. And I have to agree with Raymond that it's my best yet. The only thing that bothers me is that we don't get to personally batter down that door and carry Santa Claus out in triumph on our shoulders. I don't like the idea of sitting back and letting some cop get the glory. On the other hand, it's a bold, foolproof plan that uses our brains instead of our muscles, and it was my idea.

"We'll do it," I tell Raymond.

Late into the night we work, using the newspapers and comic books, scissors and paste, which Raymond has provided. Each word, he explains, must be cut from a different publication. That way no one will be able to trace our handwriting. I'm not sure why that is important, but that is the way it is always done in the movies.

When we are all finished, he snips out two words from the editorial page of the *Globe* and pastes them on the bottom of the letter.

"What is that?" I ask.

"Our signature," he explains. "If Mr. Harry Walker knew this letter came from three mice, he would probably throw it in the wastebasket. So I'm signing it 'Concerned Citizens.' "

I like the sound of it. It sounds respectable. One thing you have to say about Raymond, he thinks of everything.

We stand back to look over our work. Now that it is finished, I can see that this is without a doubt the best idea I ever had. When Mr. Harry Walker gets this letter, he'll send every cop in New York racing to Santa Claus's rescue.

Carefully Raymond folds the letter, puts it into an envelope, and pastes on the address. Fats gives the envelope a couple of enthusiastic licks to seal it ("Mmmmm, peppermint") while Raymond searches in his stamp collection for a Special Delivery stamp. Then, clutching the letter tightly under my arm, I'm off to mail it in the mailbox on the main floor of the store.

114

When I return, Raymond and Fats are snoring in their beds. As I crawl wearily into my own, my last thought is of a fleet of police cars, sirens wailing, roaring off to Brooklyn. In just a few hours Santa Claus will be back, and we will be heroes.

Thanks to me.

13

I Have Dreams of Glory

"And as a token of our appreciation," says the mayor, "I present to you the key to our great city. Plus a year's supply of caviar."

I am standing on the steps of City Hall with the mayor beaming on one side of me and Santa Claus looking grateful on the other.

"It was nothing really," I say modestly.

A great cheer goes up from the crowd below. A brass band starts playing, and hundreds of children stand up and throw rose petals. Then the strangest thing happens. The rose petals turn suddenly into pickles. I try to duck, but it's no use. I'm being pelted with pickles.

I open my eyes to find a pickle next to my nose. Holding it is Fats, and he looks worried.

"He's not back yet," he says. "I've been watching all morning, and Santa Claus hasn't come back."

I shove the pickle away and turn over. "Too soon," I mumble. "Our letter hasn't gotten there yet. He'll be back tomorrow."

Pulling the quilt over my head, I go back to my dreams of glory.

The next morning it's pickle juice running down my neck that wakes me up. I know right away it's Fats again. Ever since he started his Santa Claus watch, he's been nervously eating pickles non-stop.

"He's still not back," he reports. "And there are only two more shopping days until Christmas."

I sit up. This is a little strange. I thought the cops would have located Santa Claus by now.

"Maybe something went wrong," Fats suggests anxiously.

"Nonsense!" I reply. "What could go wrong? My plan was foolproof. No, we must be patient. Santa

Claus will be here any minute now."

But the minutes go by and then the hours, and our Santa Claus does not show up. That ridiculous young whippersnapper of a Santa Claus is there, telling the kids to "Have a cool Yule and a groovy New Year," but the real one is still missing.

After lunch I slip out to my listening post to see if the saleswomen have any news.

Mrs. Feldman is up on a stepladder helping Mrs. O'Grady put the bride and bridesmaid dolls on the top shelf of the display case.

"It's sad, isn't it," she says, "that Mr. Dunderhoff won't be at the office party on Christmas Eve. He always enjoyed so much handing out the gifts."

Mrs. O'Grady agrees that it's awfully sad.

"We all know it's awfully sad," I grumble. "Tell me something new." But they don't tell me anything more. A customer wants to see the bride and bridesmaid dolls, and Mrs. O'Grady climbs up to take them out of the case again.

I creep back to my house. Still hoping, I keep watch all afternoon. But as the salespeople start counting up the money in their registers, I have to admit that something has gone wrong.

"I don't understand it," I tell Raymond. "How could our plan have failed? It was foolproof."

Raymond is stitting in the rocking chair drawing little Santa Claus faces in his notebook. "I've been thinking about that," he says. "And there are two possible explanations. The letter could have gotten lost in all the Christmas mail and never reached Mr. Harry Walker. Or he could have thrown it in the wastebasket, thinking it was a hoax."

"I knew this plan of yours would never work," I mutter. "It was a dumb idea. We shouldn't have left the job to someone else."

"Or," continues Raymond, "there is one more possibility. Maybe it just hasn't gotten to Mr. Harry Walker yet. I read in the newspaper this morning that the mail is always slow at Christmas time."

This is possible, I suppose. But in my heart of hearts I know the letter is lying in Mr. Harry Walker's wastebasket, ripped into a million pieces. Our mission has failed. My career as a master detective is ended. Now I'll never receive the key to the city.

But if I am depressed, Fats is totally destroyed. He lies limply on my bed, the quilt covering all of him but his nose, looking like an unhappy vegetable.

119

"Cheer up, Fats," I tell him. "Nothing is so bad that it can't be cured by a peanut butter and watermelon-pickle sandwich."

A faint moan comes from beneath the quilt. I think maybe that was not the best suggestion. He has eaten too many pickles already.

I try pep talks, bribes, even a little torture twist applied to his tail, but nothing can make him budge. It is not until later that night that I hit on a way to cheer him up.

Quietly I slip out of our house and take the escalator direct to the furniture department. It is here in one of the model rooms that I have seen what I need. I climb up on the mantelpiece and select a branch of just the right size from a pile of evergreens. I come back with it over my shoulder.

"All right, Fats, old boy," I say. "Open your eyes."

One eye slowly opens. Then the other. Then he is bouncing up and down squealing, "A Christmas tree! A real, live, genuine Christmas tree!"

"Nothing but the best," I say. "None of this phony plastic stuff for us."

So it is that I, Merciless Marvin, find myself sitting at the kitchen table late that night stringing

120

popcorn to decorate a Christmas tree. It isn't dig-
nified. It isn't tough. But worst of all, as I sit there
listening to Raymond and Fats brimming over with
carols and good cheer, I catch myself humming.

This Santa Claus stuff must be starting to rub off
on me. For the song I am humming is "Rudolph the
Red-Nosed Reindeer."

14

I Become a Hero

I wake up early the next morning with that song still in my ears. Why can't I stop singing it? This is ridiculous. Then I realize it's not me but the loud-speaker in the toy department. There's a lot of other noise out there too. Too much for so early in the morning. I drag myself to the window to see what is going on.

The first thing I see is this fat guy in a red suit. He is sitting in the Santa Claus chair like a king on a throne, bouncing a little kid on each knee. All around him are more kids and parents and salespeople and photographers snapping pictures and saying, "Just one more, please, Santa."

Can it be him? Or am I dreaming? Cautiously I check him over from head to toe. His beard is real. His pink cheeks are real. His fat stomach is real. His smile from ear to ear is definitely real. But it's not until he pats each kid on the head and says, "Merrrrry Christmas! Ho ho ho!" that I know for sure that our Santa Claus has returned.

"Raymond! Fats!" I shout. "He's here! Santa Claus is back!"

Brushing the sleep from their eyes, they come running to hang out the window.

"I don't believe it!" Fats cries, jumping up and down. "The real, live, genuine Mr. Dunderhoff."

Raymond nods, looking pleased. "So," he says, "Mr. Harry Walker got our letter after all."

"I knew my plan couldn't fail," I tell him. "It was foolproof."

Raymond and I are so busy congratulating ourselves on the success of our mission that we don't even notice when Fats falls out the window. It is only as I am preparing to sneak out and borrow Mrs. O'Grady's newspaper to read all about our heroic

123

deed that I hear a small familiar voice calling weakly, "Help!"

I rush to the window. Far below, sprawled out on a white lace pillow in a super-deluxe doll carriage, is Fats. He couldn't have made a more perfect landing.

"Stay there," I order. "Don't move. I'm coming to get you."

I don't hurry. I figure with everyone's eyes on Santa Claus, nobody is going to notice that a mouse has taken up residence in one of the doll carriages. And even if they do, with Fats's figure, they'll think he's a stuffed mouse.

After the complications of our rescue of Santa Claus, my rescue of Fats is child's play. By noon we are both safely back in my room listening to Raymond read aloud the *New York Globe* account of our triumph.

It's on the front page this time, with a close-up picture of Santa Claus beaming at the policeman who rescued him. The headline reads: "On the Night Before Christmas, Macy's Santa Is Back."

"Read it all," I tell Raymond. "I want to hear every word."

He nods and begins:

"The strange case of the disappearing Santa
Claus was solved last night when police, acting
on a tip, rescued Hans Dunderhoff, 76, from an
apartment in Brooklyn where he had been held
captive for over a week. Mr. Dunderhoff was un-
harmed. But the solution to this unusual case
appears to be as bizarre as the crime itself. For
the man responsible for the kidnaping, according
to a statement given reporters by Detective
Joseph Billoto, is none other than the Santa
Claus employed by Macy's traditional arch-rival,
Gimbels.

"Detective Billoto said that Mr. Dunderhoff
was found in the apartment of Gimbels' Santa,
Thomas Brody, at 515 Willis Avenue. Mr.
Brody, who was asleep in the apartment when
police entered, immediately confessed to his part
in the crime. In his statement he implicated the
manager of Gimbels' toy department, James
Slattery, as the originator of the kidnaping
scheme. The motive was said to be Mr. Slattery's
fear of being fired if his department did not do a
better Christmas business than in past years.
Gimbels' president Andrew Stern, in a statement

issued this morning, expressed shock at the incident and emphasized that no other store personnel had been involved.

"Because of the popularity of Mr. Dunderhoff, who has been Macy's Santa Claus for eighteen years, the kidnaping has received wide publicity. It was the public's interest, according to Detective Billoto, which led to cracking the case. Police followed up more than seventy leads, including many calls from children. The break in the case was an anonymous letter sent to this reporter and forwarded to police, which described where Mr. Dunderhoff could be found.

"So on the morning of the night before Christmas, Santa Claus is back on the job at Macy's. He's delighted to be back and so are his coworkers. But most excited of all are the children. The looks on their faces say more than any words can how overjoyed they are that he's back in time for Christmas."

Raymond puts down the newspaper.

"It's a beautiful story," sighs Fats, wiping a tear from his eye. "So touching."

"Not bad," I agree. "There's only one thing missing. It didn't mention us."

"Of course not," says Raymond. "We signed the letter 'Concerned Citizens' because we wanted to remain anonymous."

"What's anonymous?" asks Fats.

"You tell him, Raymond," I snap impatiently.

"Anonymous means 'having or revealing no name,'" explains Raymond.

"But if they don't know our names," I reason, frowning, "how can we receive the reward? How will everyone know we are heroes?"

Raymond takes off his spectacles, blows off an invisible speck of dust, and puts them back on. "Marvin," he says, "it has unfortunately been my experience that when you are a mouse, it is best to attract as little attention as possible. Do you remember what happened to Jerome?"

I shudder. Jerome was a mouse of our acquaintance when we lived in the movie theater. One day he got tired of living a life of obscurity, sneaking around and hiding in mouseholes. Boldly he strolled to the center of the stage and, in the glare of a giant red spotlight, began performing a soft-shoe. There was one moment of glorious uproar in the theater, and then ushers closed in on him from all sides. We never saw Jerome again.

"Besides," Raymond is saying, "what reward could anyone give us that would top what we have here—our own cozy little house, entertainment each night, all the food we can eat just an escalator ride away? You said yourself it was a beautiful setup."

I have to admit this is true. What would I actually do with the key to the city?

"And anyway," Raymond concludes, "the one person who counts—Santa Claus—knows we are heroes."

Personally I wouldn't mind a little more glory than that, like maybe a parade down Broadway. But all things considered, I'm afraid Raymond is right. For a mouse, fame can be a risky thing.

"How do we know Santa Claus knows we are heroes?" I ask.

"Just wait," replies Raymond confidently.

I wait all afternoon, while outside more people than I've ever seen even in rush hour mill around waiting to see Santa Claus. Every kid in the city is here, it seems, along with parents and grandparents and store officials and reporters and photographers.

Even the mayor comes to shake Mr. Dunderhoff's hand and have his picture taken presenting him with a gold medallion "as token of the deep affection of all the children of our great city."

As Santa Claus is accepting the medallion, Fats insists that he looks up at our house and winks, but I don't see it.

When the store finally closes, the toy department still doesn't quiet down. For then the office party begins, with eggnog and fruitcake and Christmas cookies and our Santa Claus reaching into his overflowing sack to hand out gifts to everyone. The president of Macy's appears and makes a speech about how pleased he is to have Mr. Dunderhoff back. "We are everlastingly grateful," he says, "to whoever wrote that anonymous letter. I only wish the authors of it would come forward so we could thank them properly."

There it is: our last chance to claim the glory that is rightfully ours. Visions of fame and fortune dance once more in my head, and I make a move for the stairs.

"Marvin," says Raymond quietly. "Remember Jerome."

129

Reluctantly I return to the window. We watch until at last the lights are turned low, and people start heading for the escalator calling, "Good night and Merry Christmas everyone!" Santa Claus is the very last to leave. But finally he slings his sack over his shoulder and, with Mrs. O'Grady and Mrs. Feldman, walks toward the escalator. Fats waves to his back. "Good night and Merry Christmas, Santa," he whispers.

And then, almost as if he'd heard, Santa Claus stops and comes back, straight toward our house.

"Now you've done it," I growl at Fats, forgetting for a moment that Santa Claus is our friend.

As we watch from behind the curtains, he reaches into his sack, opens the front door, and slips something inside. Then, closing the door quietly, he walks away toward the escalator.

"He winked at us! This time I'm sure of it," says Fats excitedly, but the light is too dim for me to be sure.

"Never mind that," I say. "Let's see what he left us. Probably a piece of fruitcake."

The three of us race for the stairs, nearly tum-

130

bling down them in our haste. Just inside the door is a Snickers wrapper, just like he always used to leave for us. Carefully I open it. What's inside is much better than fruitcake. There, gleaming in the dim light, is the gold medallion presented to Santa Claus by the mayor of New York.

"For us?" breathes Fats in amazement.

"There's a note here too," says Raymond.

"Read it," I order.

Raymond holds it up, squinting through his spectacles. "It says: 'Thank you, my little friends, and Merry Christmas!'"

I stroke the smooth, rich surface of the medallion, then lift the ribbon and put it around my neck. Glory has found me after all. This is even better than the key to the city—I can wear it.

Suddenly I feel like celebrating. "Let's have our own party," I tell my gang.

"Hooray!" shouts Fats.

Our party goes on long into the night. After we have stuffed ourselves on leftover Christmas cookies, fruitcake, and eggnog from the office party, we gather around our own genuine Christmas tree and

Raymond leads us in a round of Christmas carols, accompanying himself on the xylophone. Even I join in for a rousing chorus of "Rudolph the Red-Nosed Reindeer." Fats, dressed up in a ridiculous red costume borrowed from a Swiss doll, performs a special Christmas version of his famous cheese dance with jingle bells around his neck and a bit of tinsel dangling from his ear.

As for me, something strange happens just as I hear the cuckoo clock in the toy department strike midnight. I suddenly feel this peculiar sensation in my throat. Kind of a choked up feeling. Is this what Raymond meant by the Christmas spirit? Or is it just a touch of indigestion?

Whatever it is, I can't help myself. I look at my gang and I say, "Merrrrrry Christmas! Ho ho ho!"

About the Author

Jean Van Leeuwen grew up in Rutherford, New Jersey. After graduating from Syracuse University, she went to work in publishing and was for ten years an editor of children's books. She is the author of a number of books for young readers, including *The Great Cheese Conspiracy,* which also features Marvin and his gang. "Irresistibly laughable," said *Kirkus Reviews* of her most recent novel, *I Was a 98-Pound Duckling,* which *Publishers Weekly* called "a witty and charming book."

Ms. Van Leeuwen lives in Manhattan with her husband, Bruce Gavril, and their two young children.

About the Artist

Steven Kellogg has written and illustrated many books, including *Can I Keep Him?,* one of *School Library Journal's* Best Books of the Year 1972; *The Mystery of the Missing Red Mitten,* which was selected for the 1975 Children's Book Showcase; and *The Island of the Skog,* which *Publishers Weekly* called "warm, charming, totally captivating."

Mr. Kellogg lives with his wife, six children, several cats, and a Great Dane in a pre-Revolutionary War farmhouse surrounded by hemlock woods in Sandy Hook, Connecticut.